Big Book of My World

With original illustrations by
Kali Stileman

tiger tales

tiger tales
an imprint of ME Media, LLC
5 River Road, Suite 128, Wilton, CT 06897
Published in the United States 2012
Originally published in Great Britain 2011
by Doubleday
an imprint of Random House Children's Books
Concept and text copyright © 2011 Random House Children's Books
Illustrations copyright © 2011 Kali Stileman
CIP data is available
ISBN-13: 978-1-58925-114-4
ISBN-10: 1-58925-114-8
Printed in China
SWT 0112

1 3 5 7 9 10 8 6 4 2

For more insight and activities,
visit us at www.tigertalesbooks.com

Original illustrations by the creator of the
tiger tales picture book *Roly-Poly Egg*

Introduction

Young children have boundless energy and a thirst for knowledge that is greater than at any other time in life. A child's world is the most exciting and interesting place to be, and this book is bursting with all of their favorite things!

Big Book of My World works on many levels to stimulate reflection and reinforce learning. The best way to use this book is by having fun exploring the key principles: naming, seeking, spotting, and explaining. Here are a few suggestions:

Counting – Point to each line of owls and count them. Ask what the owls are doing, leading up to the surprise arrival in the last line!

Shapes – Point to and name the ten key shapes. Ask your child to find them in the picture. Many of the shapes appear more than once; count them all.

Colors – Link colors to recognizable objects, developing color association. Ask children if they've ever seen the same objects in other colors, such as brown leaves, red flowers, and blue doors.

Sounds – Act out the sounds together. Ask silly questions, such as "Does a pig say moo?"

Opposites – Name other things that are opposite.

Feelings – Talk about feelings. Ask why we feel happy, sad, or other moods.

Manners – Discuss which manners are good and which are not as nice.

First Words & Can You Find? – Use these sections to help build vocabulary and recognition skills. Ask your child to name the object in the border and identify it in the main picture. Ask questions, such as "Which is your favorite place, and why?"

Favorite Things – Ask children to name which vehicles, toys, food, and animals they like best.

Activities – Play these games a variety of ways. For example, in Not Like the Others, children can find the object that's different and practice counting.

Above all, enjoy sharing the pictures and words together. Then watch children go back to the pages time and time again on their own, as they fully explore the Big World they live in.

And don't forget to find at least one owl on every spread!

Contents

FAVORITE THINGS

ACTIVITIES

Counting

Big Brother

Grandpa

Little Brother

Grandma

Big Sister

Mommy

Baby

Nana

Daddy

Granddad

The Owl Family Tree

1 2 3 4 5 6 7 8 9 10

Can you spot and name all the colors?

pink

purple

brown

white

black

Sounds

meow

choo choo

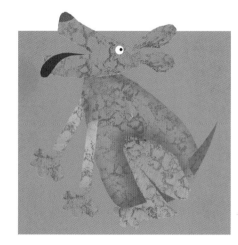

woof woof

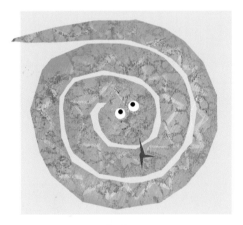

hiss

pop

buzz

ring ring

hoot hoot

pitter-patter, splash

Can you make all these sounds?

tweet tweet

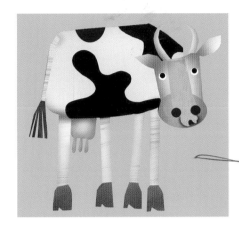

moo

squeak squeak

gobble gobble

vroom

crash

bang bang

oink

shhh

Opposites

big   small

up   down

light   dark

hot   cold

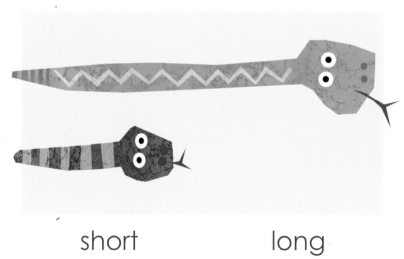

short   long

in   out

Do you know the difference between each pair of objects?

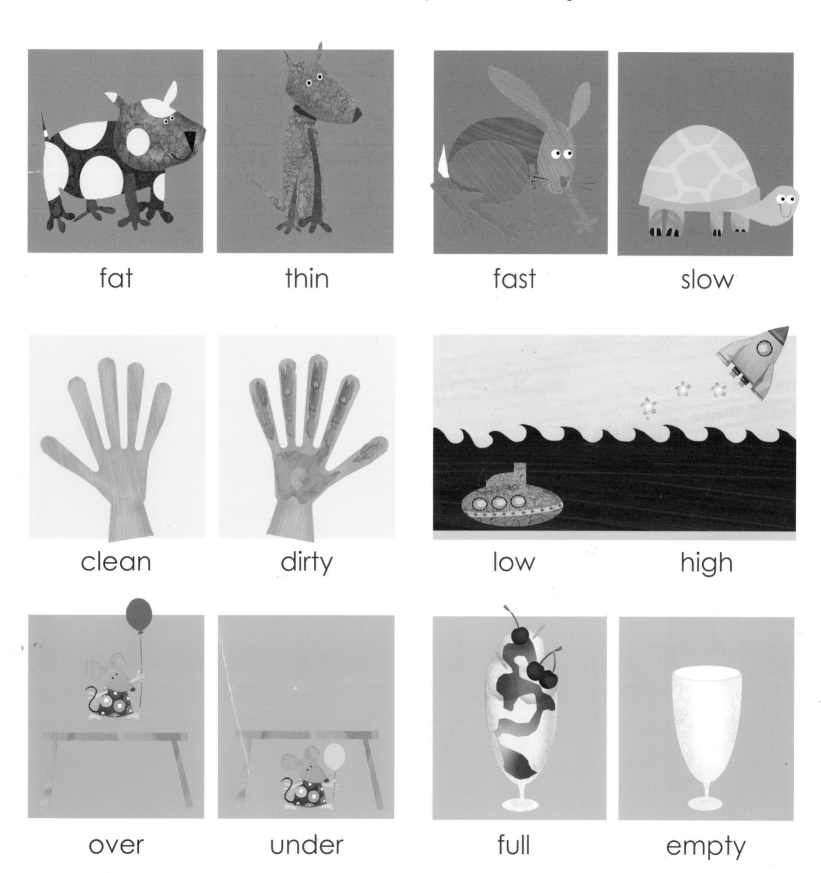

fat thin fast slow

clean dirty low high

over under full empty

Feelings

happy

love

sad

sick

shy

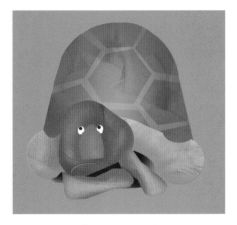

bored

scared

angry

excited

Manners

please

thank you

nice

mean

quiet

loud

sharing

tidy

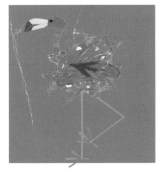

messy

grabbing

Things in the Park

bench

sandbox

pond

see-saw

jungle
gym

How many words do you know?

ducks

merry-go-round

slide

swings

tree

In the Town

house

traffic circle

tow truck

apartments

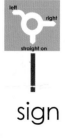

sign

Can you name the things in this town?

police car

shop

parking lot

factory

road

Out at Sea

fish

submarine

crab

jellyfish

speedboat

What do you find on the farm?

stables

dog

horse

duck pond

ducklings

sheep

fox

pig

barn

At the Beach

starfish

boat

tide pool

kite

seagull

towel

sun

ice-cream stand

What can you spot at the beach?

train

sandcastle

lifeguard

beach ball

donkey

shovel

pail

cabana

Toys

tricycle

dinosaur

paint set

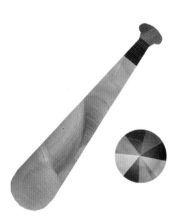

bat and ball

building blocks

doll

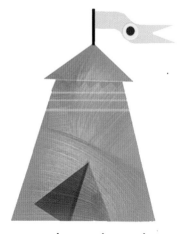

play tent

push-along dog

tool kit

What do you like to wear?

hat

pants

sweater

dress

scarf

shoes

poncho

skirt

undershirt

cardigan

underpants

tights

Trucks, Diggers,

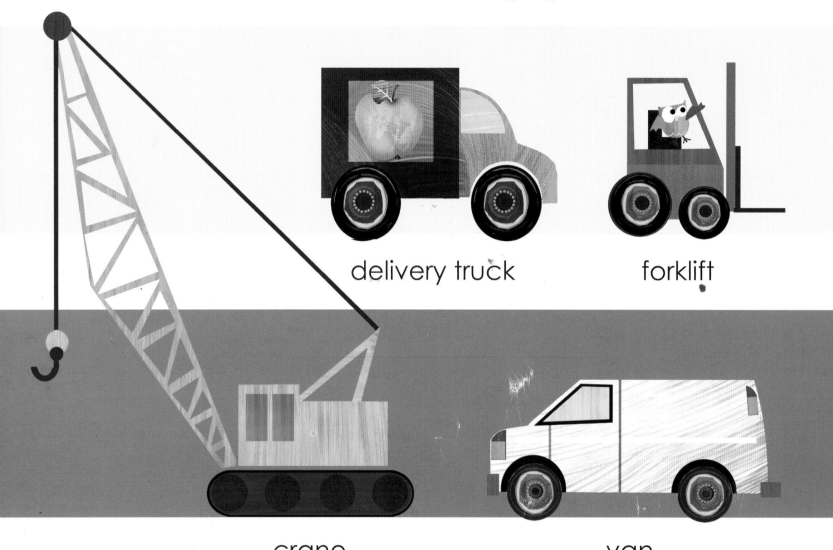

delivery truck

forklift

crane

van

fire engine

dump truck

and Big Machines

tractor

bulldozer

rocket

cement mixer

digger

tow truck

tank truck

Cars, Trains,

helicopter   car   sailboat

taxi   steam engine   bicycle

hot-air balloon   cruise ship   sports car

Planes, and Boats

motorcycle   race car   airplane

bus   police car   tugboat

train

Fruit and Vegetables

apple

orange

strawberries

pear

raspberries

kiwi

bananas

blueberries

lemon

peach

cherries

melon

grapes

mango

pineapple

plum

Have you tried any of these?
Which are your favorites?

carrots

potatoes

broccoli

asparagus

corn

leek

lettuce

tomato

celery

peas

cauliflower

pepper

onion

eggplant

Wild Animals

lion

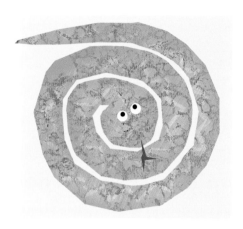

snake

elephant

rhinoceros

penguins

flamingos

sea lion

crocodile

kangaroos

Can you name all the animals?

monkeys

meerkats

giraffe

zebra

peacock

armadillo

tiger

tortoises

yak

Matching Pairs

Can you match the object to the shape?

Weather

Can you match the weather to the picture?

sunny   stormy   cloudy   rainy

hailing   snowy   windy   foggy

Seasons

Can you match the season to the picture?

autumn	spring	winter	summer

Not Like the Others

Find the one object in each line that's
not like the others.

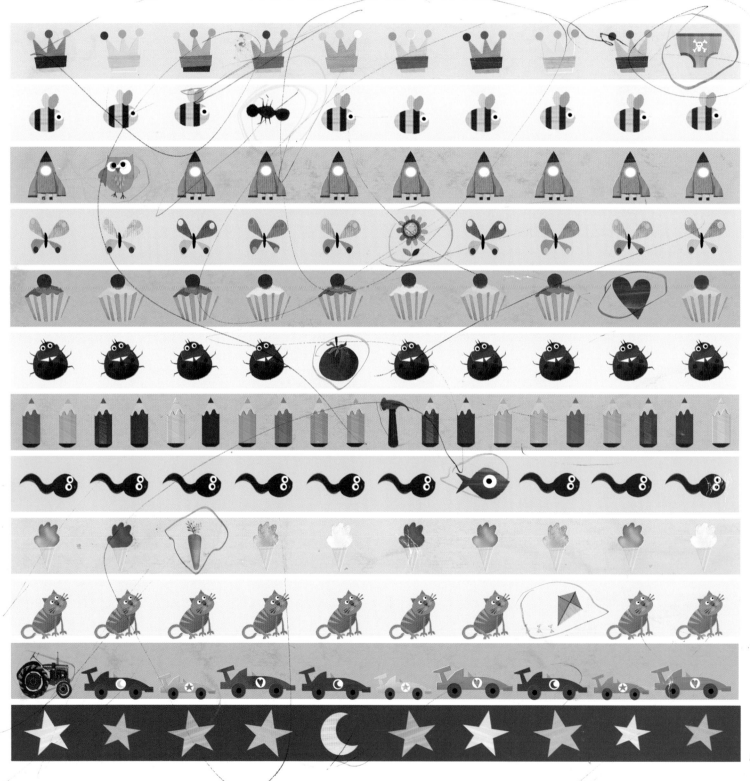